My First Trip

My First Trip to the Beach

Greg Roza

illustrated by
Aurora Aguilera

PowerKiDS
press

New York

Published in 2020 by The Rosen Publishing Group, Inc.
29 East 21st Street, New York, NY 10010

First Edition

Editor: Elizabeth Krajnik
Art Director: Michael Flynn
Book Design: Raúl Rodriguez
Illustrator: Aurora Aguilera

Cataloging-in-Publication Data

Names: Roza, Greg.
Title: My first trip to the beach / Greg Roza.
Description: New York : PowerKids Press, 2020. | Series: My first trip | Includes index.
Identifiers: ISBN 9781538345627 (pbk.) | ISBN 9781538344347 (library bound) | ISBN 9781538345634 (6pack)
Subjects: LCSH: Beaches—Juvenile literature. | Beaches–Recreational use—Juvenile literature. | Outdoor recreation—Juvenile literature.
Classification: LCC GB453 .R695 2020 | DDC 910.914'6—dc23

Manufactured in the United States of America

CPSIA Compliance Information: Batch #CSPK19. For further information contact Rosen Publishing, New York, New York at 1-800-237-9932.

Contents

My name in Noah.
Will is my best friend!

5

It is hot and sunny today.

This is my first trip to the beach!

"Let's go in the water!"
says Will.

"Wait!" says Will's mom.
"You need sunscreen!"

"Let's go!" says Will.
We run down to the water.

Will runs into the water. SPLASH!

I walk slowly into the water.

The water is warm.
We jump and splash!

That was fun! Will and I
need a rest.

"I'm hungry," says Will. "Let's have
a snack."

"Let's build a sandcastle," says Will.

Our sandcastle grows tall.

Emma wants to help build too!

"Not that way, Emma," says Will.

"Like this!"

It's time to leave. What a fun day at the beach! I can't wait to go back.

Words to Know

sandcastle

splash

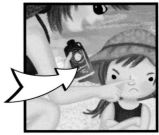
sunscreen

Index